For Archie and Morag Ann,
Charlie and Moira

First published in Dutch in 2005 by Leopold/Amsterdam
First published in English in 2006 by Floris Books

© Sandra Klaassen 2005

ISBN-10 0-86315-561-8
ISBN-13 978-086315-561-1

British Library CIP Data available

Printed in Poland

Sandra Klaassen

Uan the Little Lamb

Floris Books

Once there was a small island in the sea.
It was the most beautiful island in the world,
especially when the sun was shining.

But here on the rocky edge of the sea,
the weather was sometimes terrible.
There were gales and crashing waves.
The sky was all dark and big black clouds
rushed low as if they wanted to catch you.

And the wind was so wild ...

... it threw the sea spray high up in the air.
And everyone had to run for shelter.
Even the animals.

One year the gales seemed to go on forever.
Even springtime didn't drive away the winter weather.
We found a poor newborn lamb down on the shoreline,
abandoned by her mother.

We took the little lamb home,
all dirty and wet and shivering with the cold.

First we rubbed her dry.

Then we gave her some milk, as she was so hungry.

Then we put her in a box
so she could be warm and comfortable.
"We're going to call you Uan," we told her,
which means 'lamb' in our language.
"Be-ee-eh," said Uan.
We thought she was the sweetest little lamb we'd ever seen.

Uan must have missed her mother a lot.

So we took special care of her.

After a few days we took Uan outside.

We made a nice home for her where she could sleep and shelter from the rain.

But Uan really preferred being with us, so we took her along all the time.

We played with her and cuddled her.

As the days passed, Uan grew bigger and bigger.

Soon she had a beautiful white woollen coat.

Her little black face turned even blacker and on top of her head were two black dots.

Uan liked it when we tickled her on the nose.

She wanted to go everywhere with us.

Even to school!

After a while Uan was big enough to go out in the fields
with the other lambs.
While the mothers grazed quietly
the lambs played games together.
Uan had lots of fun.

Uan grew bigger and stronger.
She was no longer a lamb but a full-grown sheep.
Now she wanted to be with the other sheep
and she went further and further to graze.
But as soon as we called her name, she would come running up.

Summer turned to autumn, then winter, and the year came to an end.
Then another spring, summer, autumn and winter went by ...

And then ...
one spring day ...

Uan had her own sweet little lamb.

We thought she was the best mother in the world!